Hart, Charlie.
How to be a sister
without losing your mind.
2017.
33305241231442
gi   05/07/18

SISTER

without

LosinG

YOUR

MIND

CARTOON NETWORK BOOKS
an imprint of
Penguin Random House

by Charlie Hart   illustrated by Shane L. Johnson

CARTOON NETWORK BOOKS
Penguin Young Readers Group
An Imprint of Penguin Random House LLC

Penguin supports copyright. Copyright fuels creativity, encourages diverse voices, promotes free speech, and creates a vibrant culture. Thank you for buying an authorized edition of this book and for complying with copyright laws by not reproducing, scanning, or distributing any part of it in any form without permission. You are supporting writers and allowing Penguin to continue to publish books for every reader.

Photo credits: pages 69, 71: (scissor icons) © Thinkstock/da-vooda

TM and © Turner Broadcasting System Europe Limited, Cartoon Network (s17)

Published in 2017 by Cartoon Network Books, an imprint of Penguin Random House LLC, 345 Hudson Street, New York, New York 10014. Manufactured in China.

ISBN 9780451532992   10 9 8 7 6 5 4 3 2 1

My name is Anais Watterson, and as you may know, I have a great deal of experience dealing with my family members—specifically, my brothers, Darwin and Gumball. Most of the time, we get along fine, but every once in a while things can become . . . challenging.

Chances are, the reason you picked up this book is that the word **SISTER** caught your eye, and you may feel like your sibling is driving you crazy. Or maybe a well-meaning grown-up handed it to you because he or she thinks you could use a little help with being a sister. . . some "as**SIS**tance" if you will. Or it could be that you're about to become a sister very soon, and you've decided to make sure you're prepared.

Maybe you aren't a sister at all. Maybe you're a boy, but you have a sister, and you want to see what she's thinking so you can understand what makes her tick. (If so, you are nothing like my brothers, and I would like to meet you.)

Regardless of how you got this book in your hands, I am glad you are reading it.
Sincerely,
Anais Watterson

THINGS YOU WILL FIND in THIS BOOK

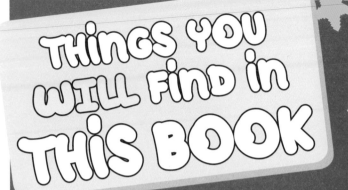

MY EXPERIENCES: I'll share stories from my own family, including the different ways I've tried to deal with Gumball and Darwin, and even Mom and Dad. Sometimes I'm smart enough to make things go my way. Other times, I feel like I should move to Neptune. Regardless, I always learn something.

TIPS: The stuff that worked? I'll pass along.

WARNINGS: The stuff that didn't work? I'll paint it red and wave it like a flag so you know not to try it.

ACTIVITIES: I'm not doing all the heavy lifting on my own, people. We're in this thing together. You'll find pages with blanks you can fill in yourself so you can tell me about your family while I tell you about mine. Also, there are pages with stuff that you can pull out and use if you're the crafty type.

QUIZZES: Don't worry! There's no grade or anything. While I personally love to take a test at school, I know it's not everyone's idea of a good time. These quizzes don't have any right or wrong answers.

CHALLENGES: No, I won't dare you to eat a worm. (Although, Darwin would probably do that just to prove he could.) These challenges are mainly about getting to know the people in your family a little better, and also getting to know yourself.

THINGS YOU WON'T FIND in THIS BOOK

One-Size-Fits-All Answers:

Every family is different, so there isn't a single right way to do anything. Take what works and leave the rest.

A Fairy-Tale Ending:

Sometimes there are hard situations in families that just can't be fixed. No matter how much I love him, Darwin is never getting any smarter.

Judgment of Any Kind:

I love my family, even when they do things I don't like. Also, I'm not perfect, but my brothers are hard enough to deal with. I'm not going to beat up on myself. You shouldn't, either.

CHAPTER 1

FACE IT: YOU'RE STUCK WITH THESE PEOPLE

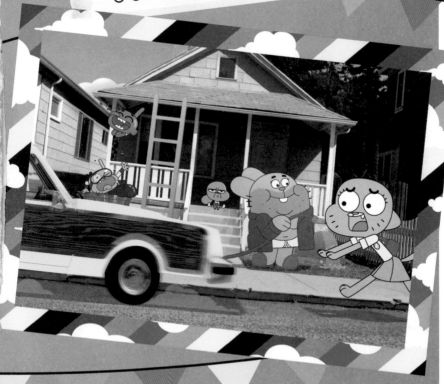

Maybe you're the oldest kid in your family, or the youngest; maybe you're smack-dab in the middle. Maybe you have a mom and a dad, or just one or the other; maybe you have two dads or two moms; maybe you live with your grandma.

Wherever you find yourself, you're part of a family, and families are forever. I know this might not be very encouraging to hear at this precise moment—especially if your brother is currently gluing your favorite sweater to the dog, or your sister has just painted a masterpiece on your homework for tomorrow. As annoyed as you might be by these people, you're stuck with them.

The dictionary defines **FAMILY** like this:

1. "A social unit consisting of one or more adults together with the children they care for."
2. "Any group of persons closely related by blood, as parents, children, uncles, aunts, and cousins."

My own grandmother has a . . . shall we say . . . **UNIQUE** personality? I'm personally very grateful she does not live with us all the time. However, maybe your grandma is great and lives upstairs. If she does, I hope she buys you ice cream and takes you to see **DAISY ON ICE**.

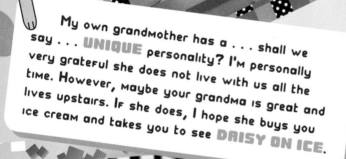

As for me, I just live with my mom and dad and my two siblings.

A sibling is a brother or sister with whom you share at least one parent. When it comes to brothers and sisters, it generally goes in one of four ways:

BIRTH SIBLING: A brother or sister born to the exact same parents you have. Same mom. Same dad.

HALF SIBLING: A brother or sister with whom you share only one parent. For instance, if your mom or dad had a baby with another person, that baby would be your half sibling because you only have one parent in common.

STEP SIBLING: A brother or sister to whom you are related by marriage. When two people who already have children get married, those kids become stepbrothers or stepsisters.

ADOPTED SIBLINGS:

If a family that already has kids adopts a child, all of those kids become siblings.

I have an adopted sibling in my very own family. My brother Gumball had a goldfish named Darwin. One day, Darwin grew legs and learned how to talk. So, my parents, Nicole and Richard, adopted him. Now, Darwin is my brother.

We don't look anything alike. I look like (a much prettier version of) my father, and Gumball takes after my mom. But Darwin is my brother just the same, and honestly, sometimes he's a lot easier to deal with than Gumball.

Some days I feel like I'm more related to Darwin than I am to Gumball. Some days, I wish I wasn't related to either of them. Some days, I am pretty sure I was left on the doorstep by aliens.

Maybe you do, too.

TIP: STAY CONNECTED!

On days when I wish I could just snap my fingers and make my whole family disappear, it helps to remember the ways that we are connected.

Here's an activity designed to help you see the connections in your family. You can do it on your own if you need a little quiet time. Or you can invite your brother or sister to help out.

ACTIVITY: MY FAMILY (BANANA) TREE

Maybe they're all a bunch of crazy apes, but you're hanging out in the same tree—at least for a few more years, anyway. Banana Joe agreed to help me out with this one. Write the names of your grandparents, parents, and siblings on the branches of this family tree.

QUIZ: WHO ARE THESE PEOPLE?

Even though you probably see your brother or sister every single day, there may be things about them that you didn't know. I sure do love a good quiz! Even though Gumball **HATES** quizzes, he took this one with me. Ask someone from your family to do this quiz with you.

On a separate piece of paper, each of you should write down your answers to the following questions. Then, take turns guessing what the other one wrote. Give yourself a point for each correct answer.

1. (1 point each) The food that will most likely make me clean my plate is ——————————. The food that makes me want to hold my nose while I choke it down is ——————————.

2. If I could choose to go to the beach or the mountains for vacation, I'd pick ——————————.

3. My favorite color is ——————————.

4. My favorite outfit or piece of clothing is ———————————.

5. If I could choose a superpower, it would be ——————————.

6. My favorite song is ——————————.

7. When I grow up, I want to be ——————————.

8. The thing my brother or sister does that makes me laugh the hardest is ——————————.

9. (1 point each) My idea of a great day is doing these three things:

———————————
———————————
———————————

10. The best book I ever read was ——————————.

HOW'D YOU DO?

8-13 POINTS

Wow! You've been paying attention. Sometimes it's easy to tune out when Gumball and Darwin are doing something crazy on the roof, but you've really been keeping your eyes peeled and your ears open. That's super because the better you know your family, the easier it is to solve problems, should they come up. (Not that they will. I'm just saying . . .)

1-7 POINTS

See? I told you your family might surprise you! Isn't it neat that people you know so well can still knock your socks off? I was stunned when I found out that Gumball had always dreamed of being a Shakespearean actor. It's great to learn more about your family because then you understand them better.

So, maybe you're stuck with these people—sometimes literally, like the time Gumball's gum wound up in his hand and then stuck to my fur. It helps to know a little bit about these people we call brothers and sisters. Knowing where I fit in my family makes me feel like I belong, and that's a good thing—especially when things get a little crazy.

CHAPTER 2

I RESIGN: MY FAMILY IS DRIVING ME NUTS

As much as I love my brothers— and I do—sometimes, they drive me bonkers.

Just last week at breakfast, I was minding my own business, looking over some vocabulary words for my spelling test. My brothers were doing something Gumball called the Bionic Breakfast Super Bowl of Champions to decide who got the last bowl of Smash-mallows cereal. Of course, I ended up getting the last bowl . . . upside down on my head.

I had to go take a shower, clean out my ears, and put on a fresh change of clothes. I was late for school and Mom had to write me a note, and I almost missed the spelling test.

You know how I feel about tests and quizzes! I love them. **DON'T MAKE ME MISS A QUIZ, GUMBALL AND DARWIN.**

Another time, Gumball and Darwin said they'd get back my Daisy the Donkey doll from some kids who'd taken it on the bus. Instead, they let Tina take her and they gave me a cheap version they tried to pass off as my real Daisy. When I pulled her string, she spoke Chinese. And then she exploded.

Maybe your brother or sister doesn't blow up your toys or spill cereal on your head. Maybe it's worse.

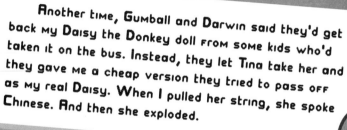

Here are the top FIVE things my brothers do that MAKE me MAD:

1. TAKE MY STUFF WITHOUT ASKING

This is not rocket science. This isn't any kind of science at all. This is something we ironed out thousands of years ago as a bedrock of civilization. If you want to use something of mine, Just ask. I'll more than likely share it with you.

2. BARGE INTO MY ROOM WITHOUT KNOCKING ON THE DOOR

A girl needs her privacy. I love to hang out with Darwin and Gumball, Just not every single second. There's even a sign on my door. It says "PLEASE KNOCK."

3. BOSS ME AROUND

Yes, I realize I'M younger than you are. That doesn't mean I'M stupid. Or that I have to do everything you say. If you ask me nicely, it might work better. After all, as the old saying goes, "You catch more flies with honey." Though why anyone would want a bunch of flies, I don't really know. I'll bet Gumball has a few ideas.

4. BLAME ME FOR SOMETHING I DIDN'T DO

Why would I throw raw eggs all over the kitchen? Yes, Gumball really told Mom that it was my fault. He said I had inspired an argument between himself and Gumball, and that a "breakfast food battle" had broken out as a result. Mom said she didn't want to hear another word, and we all had to clean up the kitchen.

5. TALK OVER ME AND INTERRUPT ME

Sometimes I feel like Gumball and Darwin are never quiet. There are times when I can't even get a word in edgewise, especially at the dinner table. Or if I'm telling Mom about something that happened to me at school that day, they just start talking when I'm right in the middle of a story. There are times I feel like I could do cartwheels down the middle of the dining room table and nobody would even see me.

What are the top five things your family does that make you get angry and lose your cool?

1. _____
_____
_____
_____
_____

2. _____
_____
_____
_____
_____

3. _____
_____
_____
_____
_____

4. _____
_____
_____
_____
_____
_____

5. _____
_____
_____
_____
_____
_____
_____
_____

When they're not making me furious, Gumball and Darwin do stuff that makes me so embarrassed I wish the ground would just open up and swallow me. Actually, I wish it would open up and swallow them.

The other day we were at Food 'N Stuff with my mom, and Gumball and Darwin decided to have a burping contest in the middle of the store. Gumball ran over to the customer service counter, grabbed the microphone from the clerk, and burped so loudly it almost blew the speakers out of the ceiling. If you have never experienced the power of amplified eructation, let me tell you: A big burp can wreak havoc on a stack of watermelons. I was so embarrassed that I climbed under the cart and hid behind the toilet paper.

I'll bet your siblings NEVER do anything that makes you shake your head in shame. (But just in case, here's a list of the things that Gumball and Darwin do. Sound familiar?)

These are the top five things my brothers do that **MORTIFY** me:

1. BURP AND PASS GAS

Sometimes I swear I am living in a wind tunnel of flatulence. It's bad enough that they smell up the whole house, but Gumball and Darwin think it's the funniest thing in the world to cut the mustard in public. And then people turn and stare, and wave their hands in front of their noses as the tears stream down from the stinky smell. Why do my brothers think this is funny?

2. TREAT ME LIKE I'M A BABY

Yes, I'm younger than they are, but I'm not helpless. In fact, I get better grades than both of them. I'm only four years old and I attend Elmore Junior High School, after all. So it makes me crazy when Gumball acts like he knows better than I do, like I'm some tiny infant who doesn't know anything. And usually, I'm just trying to keep him from doing something insane like trying to parachute off the roof with an umbrella.

3. MAKE FUN OF THE THINGS I LIKE

Yes, I love DAISY THE DONKEY. Yes, I carry my plush
Daisy doll around with me. That doesn't mean that I'm silly,
or stupid. AND DAISY ISN'T SILLY OR STUPID, EITHER.
She's smart, and funny, and makes me feel like I have a
friend all of the time.

4. ACT LIKE UNCIVILIZED CRETINS AT SCHOOL

Gumball is always running around in the hallways at school
trying to carry out some crazy scheme. Usually Darwin
isn't far behind—either helping or trying to talk him out
of it. Typically, it ends up with both of them in Principal
Brown's office, with Miss Simian freaking out. Why can't
they just be normal?

5. TALK AND CHEW WITH THEIR MOUTHS OPEN

It's bad enough at our dinner table, but in a restaurant, it's
like somebody has turned my brothers' atrocious table manners
up to eleven. (And the knob only goes to ten!) The last time
we went to Joyful Burger, Larry brought our tray to the table
and before he'd even set it down, Gumball had devoured an
entire burger like a lawn mower, talking the entire time, tiny
pieces of food from his mouth spraying all over the table, but
mainly all over Larry. I slid out of my seat and took refuge
under the table until the carnage had ended.

Things like this happen all the time at my house.
It's a wonder I stay as sane and reasonable as I do.

What are the top five most embarrassing things your family has ever done to you? Don't worry, your mortifying secrets are safe with me!

1. _____
_____
_____
_____
_____
_____

2. _____
_____
_____
_____
_____

3. _____
_____
_____
_____
_____
_____

4. _____
_____
_____
_____
_____

5. _____
_____
_____
_____
_____
_____
_____

WHO? ME?

Let's be serious: Crazy is a two-way street. Yes, I know that our siblings do stuff that drives us downright bonkers. But if I'm going to be honest (and as a general rule, I try to be honest), then I have to admit that there are some things that I do that probably make Gumball and Darwin totally bananas, too. In my own defense, I'm usually just trying to be helpful. But I know not everybody wants help. (Even when they **NEED IT!**) So, I'm trying to be better about remembering not to do some of the items I've listed below. I'm not perfect at it by any means, but I'm trying! Remember, it's all about direction, not perfection.

Stuff I know I do that annoys Gumball and Darwin:

1. TRYING TO TRICK THEM INTO DOING WHAT I WANT

Even though they drive me crazy sometimes, Gumball and Darwin really do love me. Sometimes all I have to do is make my big shiny sister eyes at them, and they're like putty in my paws. However, that usually ends up backfiring. Just the other day, I convinced them to help me fold the laundry when they were supposed to be doing their homework. I wound up getting us all in trouble, and Gumball and Darwin were really mad at me. I guess it's not nice to manipulate people—especially people who love you.

2. TATTLING ON THEM

Nobody likes a tattletale. But sometimes they get on my nerves so badly that I just lose it and yell, "Mo-o-o-o-o-o-m!" Sometimes they do get in trouble, but usually Mom just gets annoyed that we can't work it out between us and then everybody is cranky.

3. NOT SHARING WITH THEM

What can I say? I have some nice things. Sometimes Gumball and Darwin ask if they can use my art supplies or borrow a book (not to read, mind you; usually they want to smash a bug with it). I can be stingy. Once I hid the remote from the whole family so I could see DAISY THE DONKEY on TV. (It didn't turn out well.) So, I'm trying to be better about sharing. Usually, I suggest that we all do something together, but that can backfire, too, when they feel like I . . .

4. FOLLOW THEM AROUND TOO MUCH

Look, everybody needs their space, right? But sometimes my FOMO (fear of missing out) is OUT OF CONTROL. They are older, and Mom and Dad let them do stuff that I don't get to do. Lots of times, they include me, but they don't always want me tagging along, and it hurts my feelings. I'm trying not to take that personally. We all need our alone time. It makes the times we do hang out together even more fun.

5. GLOATING WHEN THEY GET IN TROUBLE

Every once in a while, Gumball will do something ridiculous. Most often, he drags Darwin into it, too. The night he tried to ask Penny to marry him and they set the backyard on fire? Yes, that was not one of his finer moments. When things like that happen, I just can't keep my mouth closed. Nobody wants to hear "I told you so," even when you did, indeed, tell them so. Usually, they can already see that you were right and don't need you to rub it in.

CHALLENGE: FOR BETTER OR WORSE

Below, there is a list of three scenarios. The first blank is an example of how you were a pest or made things more difficult for your family. The second blank is a way to make things better in those situations. Don't think too hard—just come up with the best answer that pops into your head!

Ready? Set? GO!

1. When my brother or sister asks to use something of mine, sometimes I make things worse by

————————
——————————.

Instead, I could make things better by ———————
——————————
——————————
——————————.

2. When my brother or sister is grumpy, sometimes I make things worse by ————————————.
Instead, I could cheer them up by

——————————————
——————————————.

3. When my brother or sister does something that really bugs me, sometimes I make things worse by

————————————————.

Instead, I could make things better by ——————————————

——————————————.

CHAPTER 3

STICKING WITH IT: SMART SHORTCUTS FOR SISTERS

Seeing the Signs

Some days are all smooth sailing at our house. Other times, I wake up to the sound of Mom asking Gumball how on earth his sweater wound up in the toilet. That's when I know I'd better be on the lookout. Usually, paying attention to what's going on with my siblings can help me be aware of how they might respond to things, and allows me to make good decisions. Here are the top three warning signs in our family:

1. STRESS

I can usually tell when something is bothering my brothers: Gumball gets loud and angry, and Darwin gets quiet and sulky. Stress comes in all sorts of different ways for my brothers. Maybe Gumball got in trouble at school, and my mom is upset with him about it. Maybe Darwin is feeling left out because Gumball is spending lots of time with Penny. Whatever the case, I can usually tell when Darwin or Gumball is stressed out because they get cranky, sad, or loud.

2. MESS

We live in one of the smallest houses in Elmore. There's only one bathroom, and it can get pretty crowded and cluttered. In fact, the whole house can go from sparkling clean to falling down in a matter of moments—especially when Gumball and Dad are playing pranks on each other. This makes Mom a little crazy. She works very hard during the day and nobody likes coming home to a disaster. I prefer things tidy myself, and if Darwin or Gumball has messed up my room, there are times when I think I'm going to explode.

3. TIME PRESS

Being in a hurry is always dangerous territory for the Wattersons. My father has a genetic predisposition toward tardiness in general, and Gumball is certainly a chip off the old block. Any time we're racing out the door to school, to an activity, or to run errands is always a time to be on the lookout for conflict.

Do these three problems sound familiar in your house? Remember, there's always a way to turn the ship around and defuse the situation. Here are some shortcuts I've learned to avoid conflict with Gumball and Darwin when I see the warning signs.

TIP #1: DON'T ADD TO THE STRESS!

I've learned the hard way that when Gumball or Darwin is upset about something, the last thing they want is for me to:

- Say "I told you so!"
- Beg them to play with me.
- Find something to tattle on them about to Mom.
- Sing the DAISY THE DONKEY theme song at the top of my lungs.
- Keep doing anything that is annoying them after they've asked me to stop.

Just like I sometimes have a bad day, my brothers do, too. And when I'm feeling down, or grouchy, or lonely, there are times I just want to be left alone.

MY BIG TIP: TREAT THEM LIKE YOU'D WANT TO BE TREATED!

If you're concerned about your sibling, ask one time if everything is okay, then listen! If your brother or sister just wants to be left alone, give him or her some space. If they'd like to talk, or hang out, be patient and listen! You might also suggest playing a game or taking a walk. And remember, if you get a big fat **"GO AWAY!"** don't take it personally. Just because your sibling is having a bad day doesn't mean that you have to, too.

Making art can be a great way of letting go of some stress. Draw a picture of something that makes you feel calm in the space below!

TIP #2: HELP WITH THE MESS!

I know, I know. Nobody likes to do chores. (Okay, I like to do chores. But as Gumball will remind you, I'm not normal.) The thing is that nobody likes a fight, either. Sometimes, the best shortcut is planning ahead.

TIDY UP!

Is there a way you can chip in to help keep things orderly? Start with your own room, and make sure there's a place for everything and that everything is in its place. If you don't have a place for some stuff, decide whether you need it. If you don't need it anymore, ask your mom or dad if you can donate it to charity. Or if it's old and worn out, recycle it or throw it away. If you do have stuff you need to keep, ask your parents if you can get a box, or a bin, or some shelves to help you get organized.

HELP OUT!

Maybe it's not your mess, but I know one time Gumball had to refold all of the laundry because he kept jumping off the bed into the laundry basket that Mom had worked on all day. When she saw what was happening, she made him fold all of it by himself again. I offered to help him. I actually LIKE folding laundry. It makes me feel calm inside. And Gumball was so grateful for my help that he let me watch DAISY THE DONKEY that night even though it meant he had to wait to play video games.

MY BIG TIP: BRAINSTORM TO WEATHER THE STORM

If you can work **WITH** your siblings instead of **AGAINST** them, things go much better for everyone involved.

Everyone has a favorite and a least favorite chore. Use that to your advantage when splitting the work!

Make a list of five chores you do around the house, then rank them from your favorite to least favorite. Have a sibling or other family member do the same. Then start negotiating! If you're willing to fold some extra laundry, you might just get away with never washing dishes again.

✿ _ _ _ _ _ _ _ _ _ _ _

✿ _ _ _ _ _ _ _ _ _ _ _

✿ _ _ _ _ _ _ _ _ _ _ _

✿ _ _ _ _ _ _ _ _ _ _ _

✿ _ _ _ _ _ _ _ _ _ _ _

✿ _ _ _ _ _ _ _ _ _ _ _

✿ _ _ _ _ _ _ _ _ _ _ _

✿ _ _ _ _ _ _ _ _ _ _ _

✿ _ _ _ _ _ _ _ _ _ _ _

Making chores teamwork is a great idea. Create a chart for chores that rotates each week. Maybe you can even work out a weekly reward system for completing all the work on time without any fighting, fussing, name-calling, or burning the house down!

NAME	CHORE	SUN	MON	TUE	WED	THU	FRI	SAT

TIP #3: BREATHE THROUGH THE TIME PRESS!

Nobody likes the feeling of being late. I especially hate it when I accidentally forget something in my room, and I have to run back inside with Mom calling out, "Hurry, hurry, HURRY!"

Gumball can be especially cranky in the morning when he's tired. Or, if he was up early and had a bowl of Smash-mallows, he and Darwin will be bouncing off the walls before we actually make it to the station wagon. Usually, they forget everything they need for the school day, and have to make between one and three trips back inside. Mom starts to get annoyed, and I sit there quietly panicking, watching the seconds tick away. Inside, I'm a boiling kettle about to scream: **I'M GOING TO MISS THE BEGINNING OF THE SCHOOL DAY!**

my Big Tip: BREATHE!

Take a **BIG, DEEP BREATH.** When I start having that panicked feeling inside, I realize that I'm taking on the feelings of everybody else around me: Gumball's frantic run back inside to get his backpack, Mom's growing frustration in the front seat. Those are **THEIR** feelings, not mine. A lot of times I feel so overwhelmed by this that I barely remember to breathe.

SET THE TEMPERATURE!

I try to remember to be a **THERMOSTAT, NOT A THERMOMETER.** Meaning, I want to **SET** the emotional temperature in the car, not **REACT** to the emotional temperature in the car. Basically, it doesn't do anybody any good if I start yelling "I'm going to be late!" at the top of my lungs. If anything, that just causes more commotion and makes things take even longer.

Please help Gumball and Darwin find their way to the car so we won't be LATE FOR SCHOOL!

PLAN AHEAD!

I try to be prepared for the mornings and do things I can see will help others get out the door, too. The key to smooth mornings is planning ahead the night before! I always have a little checklist for getting out the door on time. Here's a sample one that I use. You can add your own items in the blanks.

The Anais Super Sister
Night Before Checklist
☁ School bag ready!
  ○ Homework?
  ○ Folders?
  ○ Notebook?
  ○ Permission slips?
  ○ _____
  ○ _____
  ○ _____
☁ Clothes picked out!

CHEMISTRY

PHYSICS

☁ Any extra stuff ready to go!
  ○ Special projects?
  ○ Gym clothes?
  ○ Outfit for dance class/sports practice?
  ○ _____
  ○ _____
  ○ _____
  ○ _____
☁ Alarm clock set!
☁ _____
☁ _____
☁ _____
☁ _____

TALK TO MOM OR DAD!

Ultimately, you shouldn't just sit on your feelings. If you're feeling upset in the mornings (or any other time) about being in a time crunch, discuss it with one of your parents. Show them your checklist and ask if you can make a plan together as a family so that getting out the door isn't such an ordeal.

Having a hard time talking to Mom or Dad? I have some ideas about that, too!

A WORD IN EDGEWISE: GETTING YOUR MESSAGE TO MOM AND DAD

In my family, it can be hard to get a word in edgewise. Darwin is always yap-yap-yappity-yapping his face off, and, let's be honest, he typically needs more help than I do. So, usually it's fine with me that he takes up a lot of Mom and Dad's attention. It's when they aren't paying attention to him that things seem to go wrong very quickly.

That said, there are times when I need to be heard. I'm sure you feel that way, too. But how do you talk to your mom or dad about something important, or even embarrassing?

Turn the page to immerse yourself in my illustrated guide about when and how to make sure you're heard!

Like THIS, NOT THAT

CHOOSE TO SPEAK UP!

Sometimes the hardest part for me is saying anything at all. One time I was so sad about something that happened at school, I didn't want to talk about it. I just wanted to sneak away from the dinner table and hide in my room.

Sometimes, you need to be brave and just talk about your feelings even when you don't want to. Instead of staying silent, trust the people closest to you!

Like THIS, NOT THAT

Pick THE BEST Time!

Timing is everything—especially when you're bringing up something important that you really want your parent to hear. For instance, I have discovered that if my dad is busy building a canoe out of the coffee table because Gumball has stopped up the toilet trying to flush a test he failed, that is probably not the best moment to bring up something I really need to talk to him about.

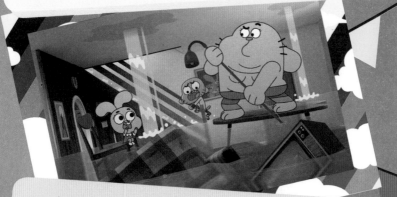

Instead, I'll wait until things are calmer around the house. Or, better yet, when I have Dad to myself in the car. Sometimes, I'll volunteer to run an errand with him, just so I have his full attention.

Like THIS, NOT THAT

MAKE AN APPOINTMENT!

It may be hard to find enough time in the day. Since I'm at school all day and Mom is working, there are days when it seems we don't have even a second alone until it's time for bed. If I bring up something important to me when I'm supposed to be brushing my teeth and getting tucked in, sometimes Mom thinks I'm just stalling.

Instead, I've learned that it's better to make an appointment with Mom. That way I know I have her complete focus when I'm talking to her.

Like THIS, NOT THAT

SLOW AND STEADY!

When I'm really excited I tend to let it all come spilling out at once. It can be really hard to understand me when I'm talking too fast and too loudly!

When I'm mad about something, I can get a little too loud! It helps if I really think about what I want to say before I open my mouth.

Like THIS, NOT THAT

PUT IT ALL TOGETHER!

The best way to be heard is to know what you want to say, pick the right time and place, and then speak slowly and thoughtfully. It's hard to get your point across when you're too excited or mad. No one wants to listen if they're afraid they're going to get yelled at.

Remember, being heard isn't just about what you have to say, it's about how you say it.

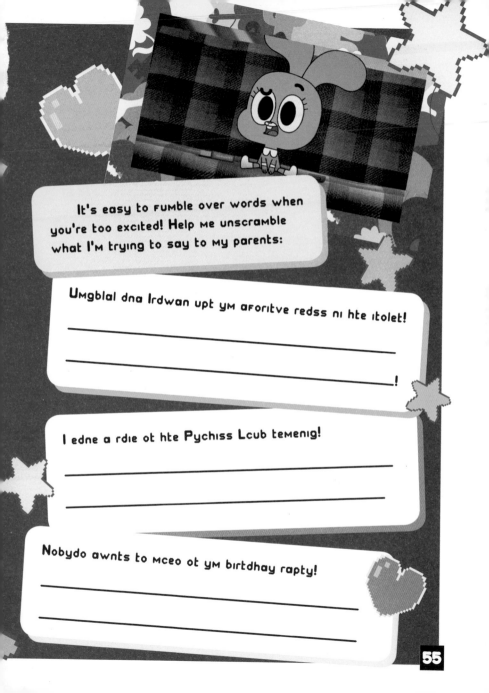

It's easy to fumble over words when you're too excited! Help me unscramble what I'm trying to say to my parents:

Umgblal dna Irdwan upt ym aforitve redss ni hte itolet!

_____

_____!

I edne a rdie ot hte Pychiss Lcub temenig!

_____

_____

Nobydo awnts to mceo ot ym birtdhay rapty!

_____

_____

THE TATTLE BATTLE

Anybody who has a brother or a sister knows how easy it is to yell "MOM!" every time your sibling does something you don't like. But the problem with tattling is that the more you do it, the less effective it becomes. I used to tell on Gumball and Darwin all the time, but Mom eventually told me that I needed to figure out on my own how to handle the little things my brothers do that annoy me.

Since then, I've been trying my best to only tell on Gumball and Darwin when they are in grave physical peril. This happens more than you might imagine. Still, I've gotten very good about figuring out when to tell on them, and when not to. I know Mom and Dad appreciate this, and it makes my relationship with Gumball and Darwin more fun, too. They don't think of me as a crybaby who is out to get them now.

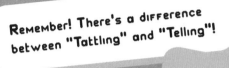

Remember! There's a difference between "Tattling" and "Telling"!

TATTLING

is squealing on your sibling every time he or she breaks even a tiny rule so that they will get in hot water with Mom or Dad. Tattling is all about getting someone else in trouble.

TELLING

is sharing information with your mom or dad when you think that your sibling may be (or might be putting someone else!) in real danger. Telling is all about keeping someone from being hurt.

QUIZ: HOW TO TELL IF I SHOULD TELL

Sometimes, Darwin and Gumball (especially Gumball) do stuff that makes me crazy, but not crazy enough to send one of us to the hospital. Other times, they do stuff that is downright unsafe.

When should I tell Mom and Dad, and when should I figure out a solution on my own? Circle the solution you think is best below, and then check your answers!

1. Darwin won't let me take a turn playing video games.

WORK IT OUT ON MY OWN

TELL MOM OR DAD

2. Gumball is trying to make a fire torch in the backyard with the lighter fluid from the grill and a stick he wrapped in an old pillowcase.

WORK IT OUT ON MY OWN

TELL MOM OR DAD

3. Darwin and Gumball are trying to hotwire the station wagon in order to go pick up a pizza for dinner.

WORK IT OUT ON MY OWN

TELL MOM OR DAD

4. Gumball keeps saying that my **DAISY THE DONKEY** sweatshirt looks silly.

WORK IT OUT ON MY OWN

TELL MOM OR DAD

5. Darwin is singing at the top of his lungs, running up and down the hallway while I'm trying to do my homework.

6. Gumball has written numbers on eighteen softballs and put them all into the dryer so he can sell lotto tickets to the neighborhood kids.

WORK IT OUT ON MY OWN

TELL MOM OR DAD

WORK IT OUT ON MY OWN

TELL MOM OR DAD

7. Gumball is trying to convince Darwin to get Penny's answers to a school project so he can copy them. He won't listen when I tell him that's cheating!

WORK IT OUT ON MY OWN

TELL MOM OR DAD

HOW'D YOU DO?

1. WORK IT OUT ON MY OWN: Instead of running to Mom every time Darwin won't let me have a turn on the video game, I've learned to go do something else. Sometimes I read a book, or use my art supplies to draw or paint a picture. Lots of times Darwin will see what I'm doing and just come join me. Then I can talk to him about letting me take a turn with the video game.

2. TELL MOM OR DAD: I'm all for building fun stuff in the backyard, but any time lighter fluid and actual fire are involved with Gumball, it's a recipe for disaster. I don't want him to blow himself up.

3. TELL MOM OR DAD: No one should be driving a car until they have a license—even if it's to surprise Mom with dinner. My brother could have a wreck and hurt himself or some innocent passerby minding her own business on the sidewalk.

4. WORK IT OUT ON MY OWN: Even though it's no fun to be teased, I know that Gumball is probably just bored or feeling bad about himself when he puts me down. Instead of yelling downstairs for Mom to make him stop, I take a deep breath and make a funny face at him. "I'll show you SILLY," I say, then race in and tickle him until he can't do anything but laugh along with me. Then I can ask him if he wants to ride bikes with me. Usually, distracting Gumball when he teases me is not very hard.

5. WORK IT OUT ON MY OWN: Darwin doesn't have the greatest voice in the world, but usually if I close my bedroom door I can still concentrate. If he's still too loud, I ask him if he can help me with a question on my math homework. Darwin likes to feel smart, and usually this will distract him from singing long enough that I can get my homework done. (He doesn't have to know that I didn't really need his help.)

6. TELL MOM OR DAD: Any time Gumball is using a major household appliance for a purpose other than the use intended by the manufacturer, I have found that it's a good idea to alert my parents. Softballs in the dryer, the neighbor's hamster in the washer, any sort of metal in the microwave . . . You get the idea.

7. TELL MOM OR DAD: I know Gumball always means well, but sometimes he only means well for himself. When I can't talk him out of a bad idea like cheating, or drinking old paint out of a can in the garage to turn himself into a superhero, I always tell Mom or Dad about it. I don't want him to get into even bigger trouble at school for cheating—or wind up in the hospital.

CHALLENGE: HOW ABOUT YOU?

Have you ever tattled on your brother or sister? List two different times you may have tattled and a way that you might be able to solve the problem on your own in the future!

1. One time, I tattled on _____ because _____ _____ _____ _____.

I could've probably solved the problem on my own if I had done this instead: _____ _____ _____.

2. One time, I tattled on _____ because _____ _____ _____ _____.

I could've probably solved the problem on my own if I had done this instead: _____ _____ _____.

CHAPTER 4

GREAT STUFF ABOUT THESE GOOBERS

SIBLING SUPERSTARS!

Sure, sometimes my brothers make me want to run screaming to the backyard. But most of the time, they're hilarious and fun. Here are the top ten things that I love about Darwin and Gumball:

10. They make me laugh.

9. Gumball is good at helping me think outside the box.

8. Darwin always knows when I need a hug.

7. We're a really good team when it comes to dinosaur abatement.

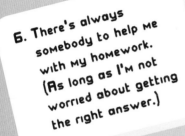

6. There's always somebody to help me with my homework. (As long as I'm not worried about getting the right answer.)

5. They remind me not to take things too seriously. Especially MYSELF.

4. They always walk me home from school.

3. Darwin always finishes the green beans I don't want.

2. Gumball is good at bedtime stories.

1. They love me no matter what.

CHALLENGE: THINGS I LOVE LIST

Set a timer for one minute. Write the name of your brother or sister in the blank at the top of this activity. On the lines beneath, list as many things as you can think of that you LOVE about your sibling. Have more than one sibling? You can do this again on a separate sheet of paper!

Ready? Set? Go!

Things I Love About _____
(Write the name of your brother or sister here.)

1. _____
_____
_____
_____

2. _____
_____
_____
_____

3. _____
_____
_____

4. _____
_____
_____
_____

5. _____
_____
_____
_____

6. _____
_____
_____
_____
_____

7. _____
_____
_____
_____

8. _____
_____
_____
_____

9. _____
_____
_____

10. _____
_____
_____
_____

HOW'D YOU DO?

I THOUGHT OF 1–5 THINGS IN A MINUTE: That's great! Maybe there are other things to love about your sibling that you just don't know about yet. Try doing the **Who Are These People?** quiz on page sixteen to find out other things about them to add to this list!

I THOUGHT OF 6–10 THINGS IN A MINUTE: Wow! It sounds like you have a great brother or sister and you know it! Does he or she know you feel that way?

ACTIVITY: SIBLING SURPRISE!

Cut out the cards on the following page and write a message to one of your siblings or another family member. Tell them what you like about them and why. Then, find a way to surprise them with it. (Under her pillow? In his book bag or lunch box? Inside a sneaker?)

Dear _____,
(Write the name of a family member here.)
Surprise! I just wanted to tell you how much I like these things about you:

1. _____
2. _____
3. _____

There are lots of other reasons I love you, too. If you want to hear about them, come and find me.

Love,

_____
(Sign your name here.)

Dear _____,
(Write the name of a family member here.)
Surprise! I just wanted to tell you how much I like these things about you:

1. _____
2. _____
3. _____

There are lots of other reasons I love you, too. If you want to hear about them, come and find me.

Love,

_____
(Sign your name here.)

Dear _____,
(Write the name of a family member here.)
Surprise! I just wanted to tell you how much I like these
things about you:

1. _____
2. _____
3. _____

There are lots of other reasons I love you, too. If you
want to hear about them, come and find me.

Love,

_____

(Sign your name here.)

Dear _____,
(Write the name of a family member here.)
Surprise! I just wanted to tell you how much I like these
things about you:

1. _____
2. _____
3. _____

There are lots of other reasons I love you, too. If you
want to hear about them, come and find me.

Love,

_____

(Sign your name here.)

STUFF YOU CAN ONLY DO TOGETHER

Let's face it: Without siblings, there's a whole bunch of cool stuff that's hard to do (except maybe with close cousins). Here are my favorite things to do with Darwin and Gumball. Maybe you can try them, too!

1. PLAYING BOARD GAMES

I know, I know. As Gumball likes to say, "A BOARD GAME? Didn't you mean a BORED game?" But I like them, and Darwin is always up for a game of checkers. And guess what? You can't play a game of checkers by yourself.

2. PLAYING HIDE-N-SEEK

If nobody is coming to find you, there's really no point in hiding, is there? This is my favorite game to play outside during the summer in our backyard or down the street at the park. Especially just before it gets dark!

3. GETTING PUSHED ON A SWING

Sure, I guess you can pump your arms and legs to make yourself go high on the swings. But I just never seem to go quite as high as when Gumball gives me a push.

4. PUTTING ON A SHOW FROM THE DRESS-UP BOX

What? You don't have a dress-up box? Well, this is the first thing to fix. We like to go to garage sales or the thrift store and get old, silly clothes: a fancy dress from thirty years ago, a cowboy hat, or a pair of forest ranger boots. After Mom washes them, we keep all of the costumes in a big bin in the upstairs closet.

You should see what the three of us come up with when we put our heads together. Last week, we put on a full circus for Mom and Dad. Now there's something you can't do by yourself!

5. SHARING SECRETS

What good is a secret without someone to share it with?

MAKING IT EASY

There are lots of things that make being a sister hard. Here are some little things I like to try to do that make being a sister easy!

1. SHARE

You know how nice it feels when your brother or sister gives you half of the cookie? Or lets you take a turn playing the video game? Or lets you throw the ball for the dog? Or lets you wear the sweater Grandma gave him for his birthday?

No?

Maybe that's because YOU never share. Somebody always has to go first.

Maybe you share all of the time, and you think your brother or sister never does. Well, you can do things the easy way or the hard way. If arguing is your idea of a great Friday night, then have at it.

Just remember, the way it feels when somebody shares with you? Your brother or sister feels that, too, when YOU share with them.

2. Help

Sometimes I try to help Gumball, but instead I just get bossy and exasperated. That doesn't help anybody at all. What Gumball really hates are chores.

Every once in a while, I can find a little space down at the bottom of my heart to help him. Not for money, or for candy, or his promise to take me to the moon on the rocket he intends to buy one day. Just because.

You should try it sometime, if you can bear it. It might work out as well for you as it does for me.

3. Listen

There are times when Darwin seems like he will never stop talking or singing. Sometimes he sings and sings and talks and talks and sings.

One day, Darwin stood in my doorway and kept talking to me. He was interrupting one of my favorite parts of the day: homework! I got so frustrated, I almost yelled, "DARWIN! BE QUIET! YOU'RE DRIVING ME BANANAS!"

But as soon as I saw how excited he was, I decided to just listen. At first it felt like my ears might fall off, but I took a deep breath. And you know what? If I hadn't listened, I wouldn't know that Darwin really likes pineapple on his pizza. And now, I know him just a little bit better.

4. COMPLIMENT

Compliments are like jumping jacks: They're easy, but I don't do them very often. I'm trying to change that.

It makes me feel good when Gumball tells me that I'm smart. I realize that I think nice things about my brothers, but I don't say them out loud very often. So I'm trying to get better at that.

"Gumball, you're very creative."

"Darwin, you have excellent concentration."

See? That's not so hard.

5. GIVE SPACE

Sometimes when I'm bored, I try to get involved in what Darwin and Gumball are doing. Most of the time, they will include me. Sometimes, though, they need alone time. Having siblings is all about knowing when to entertain yourself. And lots of times when I start doing something I find fun on my own, they'll come join me!

CHALLENGE: MAKING IT EASY EXPERIMENT

Pick one of the things from this Making It Easy list and try it with your brother or sister. How did it go? Write down what happened here:

WHEN I TRIED TO:
(Circle one!)

SHARE

HELP

LISTEN

GIVE SPACE

COMPLIMENT

WITH: _____
(Write the name of your brother or sister here.)

THIS IS WHAT HAPPENED:

THIS IS HOW I FELT ABOUT IT:

Weird & Wonderful

Families: Are they easy? Nope.
Are they fun? Sometimes!
Being a good sister is a lot like being a tree in a windstorm: You have to bend a little or you'll break! I hope this book has helped you feel a little bit more flexible and stretchy—and even closer to your very own weird and wonderful family.

Answer from page 45: